For Gillian and Eric Hill

Also by David McKee
Elmer
Elmer and Rose
Elmer and the Hippos
Elmer and the Rainbow
Elmer's Special Day

American edition published in 2011 by Andersen Press USA, an imprint of Andersen Press Ltd.
www.andersenpressusa.com

First published as *Elmer and Papa Red* in Great Britain in 2010 by Andersen Press Ltd.,
20 Vauxhall Bridge Road, London SW1V 2SA.
Published in Australia by Random House Australia Pty.,
Level 3, 100 Pacific Highway, North Sydney, NSW 2060.

Distributed in the United States and Canada by
Lerner Publishing Group, Inc.
241 First Avenue North
Minneapolis, MN 55401 U.S.A.
www.lernerbooks.com

Color separated in Switzerland by Photolitho AG, Zürich.
Printed and bound in Singapore by Tien Wah Press.
David McKee works in gouache.

Library of Congress Cataloging-in-Publication Data Available.
ISBN: 978-0-7613-8088-7
1 – TWP – 3/7/11
This book has been printed on acid-free paper.

ELMER'S
CHRISTMAS

David McKee

Elmer, the patchwork elephant, smiled. It was two days before the annual visit of Papa Red. The young elephants were excited.

"Take them for a walk, Elmer," said an older elephant. "Then we can prepare the presents in peace."

"Come on, youngsters," Elmer called. "We'll go and get the tree."
Squealing with laughter, the young elephants hurried after Elmer.

"Are we going where Papa Red lives?" they asked.
"Close by," said Elmer.
"Have you seen him, Elmer?"
Elmer smiled. "Yes," he said. For the rest of the walk,
they asked Elmer about Papa Red.

The walk went up and up. The jungle became pine trees. Then, for the first time in their lives, the youngsters saw snow. Papa Red was forgotten.

Elmer left the young ones to play in the snow and
went to choose a tree. "Hello, Elmer," said a moose.
"Let the young elephants see Papa Red tomorrow, but
keep them hidden. We'll have a busy night ahead."
"I know," said Elmer. "We won't bother you."

Elmer chose a tree that would be easy to put back later.
The youngsters helped to carry it. By now it was late.
"Straight to bed when we get home," said Elmer. "We
have a lot to do tomorrow."

The next day, everyone helped decorate the tree.
"The presents, the presents!" shouted the
young elephants.

The presents, wrapped and decorated, were placed around the tree. When it was finished, the other animals came to admire it.
"Wonderful," they said.

That night, when the big elephants were asleep, or pretending to be, Elmer collected the youngsters together. "This is your chance to see Papa Red," he said. "Hide where you can see but not be seen."

The youngsters had just hidden when, from out of the sky, came six moose, pulling a sleigh with Papa Red aboard. They landed, and Elmer helped load the presents into the sleigh. "Thanks, Elmer," said Papa Red. Then he winked. "I'm glad we weren't seen."

Papa Red flew off,
and the young ones rushed out.
"We saw him, we saw him!" they shouted. "He
took the presents." Elmer laughed and said, "This is
the season for giving. We give and Papa Red takes the
presents to whoever needs them the most."

Once all the elephants were finally asleep, Elmer
tiptoed among them. By each young elephant, he
placed a present that Papa Red had left for them.
Elmer smiled. "Good old Papa Red," he said.